Daisy Meadows

To Poppy & Jazz

Special thanks to Karen Ball

ORCHARD BOOKS

First published in Great Britain in 2021 by The Watts Publishing Group

1 3 5 7 9 10 8 6 4 2

Series created by Working Partners Limited

A CIP catalogue record for this book is available from the British Library.

ISBN 978 1 40836 384 3

Printed and bound in Great Britain by Clays Ltd, Elcograf S.p.A.

The paper and board used in this book are made from wood from responsible sources.

Orchard Books
An imprint of Hachette Children's Group
Part of The Watts Publishing Group Limited
Carmelite House
50 Victoria Embankment
London EC4Y 0DZ

An Hachette UK Company

www.hachette.co.uk
www.hachettechildrens.co.uk

Contents

Aisha and Emily are best friends from Spellford Village. Aisha loves sports, whilst Emily's favourite thing is science. But what both girls enjoy more than anything is visiting Enchanted Valley and helping their unicorn friends, who live there.

Rosymane is the first of the Healing Crystal Unicorns, whose magical lockets help to keep all the creatures of Enchanted Valley feeling well.

Firebright's special healing magic looks after the inside of the body – everything from a cold to a tummy ache.

Twinkleshade's healing crystal has the power to soothe worries away and help everyone feel calm.

Ripplestripe uses her amazing magic to heal the heart. She helps to mend friendships after arguments.

Spellford
Enchanted Valley

Enchanted Cottage
Golden Palace

An Enchanted Valley lies a twinkle away,
Where beautiful unicorns live, laugh and play.
You can visit the mermaids, or go for a ride,
So much fun to be had, but dangers can hide!

Your friends need your help – this is how you know:
A keyring lights up with a magical glow.
Whirled off like a dream, you won't want to leave.
Friendship forever, when you truly believe.

Chapter One
Welcome to Pillow Plains!

Emily and Aisha walked along the top of the crumbling brick wall outside the house where Aisha lived – Enchanted Cottage. Treading carefully, they held their arms out for balance.

"This is great practice for gymnastics," said Aisha, thinking of her favourite sport.

The sun was shining through the trees, and Emily spotted a perfect cluster of ripe cherries right above her. "Don't they look delicious?" she said to Aisha, pointing up.

"Ooh, can you reach them?" Aisha asked.

Emily reached up as high as she could. "Whoah – whoooaaaa – OH!"

In a tumble, she fell on to the lawn, rolling in the grass.

"Are you all right?" Aisha called, leaping down beside her friend to reach out a hand. Emily grasped her fingers and pulled herself up to standing, brushing the grass off her blue trousers.

"I'm fine!" Honestly, Emily wasn't too bothered – she didn't think she'd hurt herself at all.

"No, look, you're injured," Aisha pointed at Emily's elbow.

Emily looked down and sure enough, a bright red scrape had appeared.

"Maybe I should get you a plaster," said Aisha.

But as she turned to go into the house,

Emily cried out. "Aisha!"

"What is it?" Aisha asked. "Does it hurt?"

"No, it's not that. Look, my pocket is glowing." Emily reached into her trouser pocket and pulled out a glowing crystal keyring shaped like a unicorn.

Aisha dug out her identical keyring from her shorts pocket. It was glowing too. "Oh, wow!" she gasped. "It must be Queen Aurora, calling us back to Enchanted Valley!"

The girls shared a smile. Enchanted Valley was a special secret they shared. It was a wonderful place where unicorns, pixies, dragons and all sorts of other magical creatures lived. The girls held

the keyrings together so that the horns touched and immediately, coloured sparkles exploded all around them and they were lifted into the air.

A moment later, their feet came down to rest on soft grass and the sparkles disappeared around them like a melting cloud. A castle with twisty golden turrets like unicorn horns sat in the distance – Queen Aurora's home.

The girls felt a thrill of excitement. They were back in Enchanted Valley!

A tiny figure trotted out from beneath one of the golden turrets and clip-clopped across a drawbridge – it was Queen Aurora herself, come to welcome them! Her coat shone with all the colours of a sunrise – pink and purple, orange and red. The queen dipped her horn in a familiar greeting.

"Oh, thank you both for coming!" she cried. "It's so good to see you."

"How can we help?" Emily asked.

"Well, we have a visitor arriving soon," Queen Aurora explained.

"It's not Selena, is it?" Aisha said, panicking. Selena was a horrible unicorn who wanted to steal Aurora's crown and rule Enchanted Valley herself. Fortunately,

Emily and Aisha had been able to help their friend protect her kingdom.

Queen Aurora gave a gentle tinkle of laughter. "No, not Selena," she said. "It's the Crystal King. A unicorn who rules Crystal Valley, the kingdom next to ours. He's coming to see us!"

"A Crystal King!" Emily gasped. This was a whole new surprise. "What is HIS home like?"

Queen Aurora smiled. "You would love to see it – and maybe one day, you will. Though it's next to Enchanted Valley it takes a long time to get there. There are beautiful crystals, sparkling as far as the eye can see, and the kindest creatures ..." She dipped her head. "I think you girls would fit in well there."

Aisha couldn't wait to meet their new friend. "That sounds wonderful – will he bring some crystals with him?"

Queen Aurora laughed again. "Maybe! I'm glad you're excited. Even if you can't go to Crystal Valley now, I knew you'd want to be here to meet him."

The girls wouldn't have missed this for the world! But then Aisha saw Emily wince slightly as she bent her scraped elbow.

"Oh, Queen Aurora, can you help us? Emily hurt her elbow." Aisha pointed at the injury, even though Emily tried to hide it by covering her elbow with the other hand.

"It's nothing!" Emily said cheerily, but Aisha could tell her friend was in pain.

"Oh, you should have said so," the queen said. "Of course I can help. Come on!" She waved her horn over a shoulder. "Climb up!"

The girls scrambled on to her back, Aisha helping Emily. Then Queen Aurora rose into the air, cutting a path across

fluffy white clouds. They travelled over Enchanted Valley, the sun lighting their way, and came to land on a tumbling hillside covered in a patchwork of fields. A stream snaked between the fields like a length of blue ribbon. Each field was a different colour, from pink to buttery yellow, violet to the deepest blue. It reminded Aisha of the quilt on her grandma's bed, only this was a real, living colourful blanket!

As the girls looked closer, they could see that the fields were … *bouncy?* In each field, creatures tumbled and leapt, turning somersaults in the air, giggling with delight as they rose and fell, rose and fell. Their voices carried over to the girls.

"Wheeeee!"

"Boing!"

"The fields are like giant trampolines," Aisha gasped, gazing around. Just as she spoke, a little featherhog turned a dramatic loop-the-loop through the air, tail feathers flying.

"That's right." Queen Aurora smiled as a sleep pixie zoomed through the air, diving into a purple field, only to spring right back up again and shoot past their noses. "Welcome to Pillow Plains!"

Aisha couldn't see any plasters anywhere. "It looks super fun," she said. "But how will this help Emily's hurt elbow?"

"Ah, well, I need to introduce you to

someone." Queen Aurora nodded over to a corner of a field and a figure separated from the others, trotting over to greet them. It was a unicorn, with a pale pink body that deepened to a bolder pink across her mane and tail.

"This is Rosymane. She is one of the Healing Crystal Unicorns," the queen told them.

"We're very pleased to meet you," said

the girls, and Rosymane dipped her nose in greeting – it looked as soft and velvety as a marshmallow! Aisha could see a little pink crystal nestled inside a gold locket around her throat.

The unicorn blinked as she spotted the scrape on Emily's elbow. "I have just the thing for that!" As she reached round for her backpack, slung between her shoulders, Queen Aurora explained to the girls.

"Rosymane heals cuts and bruises. That's why she lives here at Pillow Plains."

"Ouch!" A sudden cry came from the corner of a yellow field as a tiny vampster tumbled into the gate. He rubbed his leg as his wings fluttered above his shoulder blades. He was a hamster, with tiny vampire wings and little fangs poking out of the corners of his mouth.

"As you can see, quite a few bumps happen here," said Rosymane.

Rosymane daintily held a pink crystal between her teeth. She carefully lowered her head to touch the crystal to Emily's hurt elbow. *Whoosh!* A little cloud of sparkles appeared and then faded away to reveal that the scrape had gone … to be replaced with shiny, pink skin. Emily rubbed her elbow.

"That's amazing!"

Chapter Two
Bouncing into Friends

Emily looked down at the skin that moments ago had had a scrape. There was no scab or scar or anything!

"How did you do that?" Emily always wanted to know the science behind things.

Rosymane smiled modestly. "It's the

magic of the lockets," she said.

"Her special talent," added the queen, looking at Rosymane fondly.

The vampster came running over. Rosymane touched her crystal to his knee and he scampered off, throwing himself into a forward roll. "Vank you, Rosymane!" he called back.

A shape appeared on the horizon, and then another and another.

"It's the other Healing Crystal Unicorns!" Queen Aurora said. "I asked them to come here, so we could all meet the Crystal King together."

The three unicorns came down to land in one of the fields and bounced towards the girls, Aurora and Rosymane.

"Hi, Rosymane! Hello, Queen Aurora!" said one of the unicorns. She had a red and orange coat that rippled with light like the glow of candles on a birthday cake. "And … are you two Emily and Aisha? We've heard so much about you!"

They'd heard about the girls? The two friends could hardly believe it. Emily reached for Aisha's hand and squeezed it.

"Yes, we are," she said, shyly.

The unicorn beamed at them. "It's an honour to meet you!"

"This is Firebright," Rosymane said. "She heals the inside of the body – anything from a cold to a tummy ache."

"I wish I'd met you last week," Emily said, rubbing her tummy. "I ate too much popcorn at the cinema!"

Everybody laughed.

Rosymane pointed her horn at a purple unicorn. "And this is Twinkleshade."

As Twinkleshade edged over to them, Aisha felt her mind clear of all her homework worries. "You heal the mind!" Aisha cried.

"That's right," Twinkleshade said.

"And finally, this is Ripplestripe, who heals the heart of any heartache, like sadness, or an argument with loved ones," Rosymane finished, as a stripy blue unicorn stepped forward.

Emily reached out to stroke Ripplestripe's blue mane gently. She didn't think she'd ever heard of a job as wonderful as that before.

"Outside, inside, head and heart – you cover it all!" Emily said.

"That's right," Rosymane said, nodding. "We have a healing crystal for almost everything." She nudged her little pink crystal over to Emily. "You two can share that crystal," she said. "Every family in the valley has four crystals. They're like a magical first aid kit!"

"How perfect! That makes total sense!" Emily said, picking up the heart crystal and slipping it into her pocket. She knew there was a reason she'd worn trousers with big pockets today!

"Now, we still have a little time before the Crystal King arrives, so would you like to have a go on the trampoline?" Queen Aurora asked.

"Yes, please!" Aisha cried, speaking for both of them. They ran through the gate to the nearest field – a pink one. It felt so soft and pillowy beneath them. Running was hard, but bouncing was easy!

"Forward roll!" Aisha cried, throwing herself into a leap. Emily did the same and the two of them rolled over and over, the field springing up under them.

The girls climbed to their feet and began to jump, holding hands as they rose higher and higher.

"Be careful!" came a cry from nearby.

They looked down to see a creature that looked like a small kangaroo with a unicorn horn.

"Hello!" Emily called. The girls both waved at him.

The kangaroo was bouncing too, but he wasn't going very high.

"I'm ..." – *bounce!* – "Springer" – *bounce!* – "the kangacorn! Nice to" – *boing!* – "meet you!"

"Nice to meet you, too,"

Emily gasped. Being on a trampoline was hard work! They clambered over to the edge of the field, with their new kangacorn friend staying close to their side. Every time someone bounced too close to them his nostrils flared and he cried out "Stay back!" or "Don't come too close." When they finally reached the gate, he let out a sigh of relief. "Thank goodness for that."

"Don't you like trampolining?" Aisha asked – she would have thought an animal that was part kangaroo would love jumping.

"Oh, I *like* it," Springer said. "Just not too much of it. I don't want to get hurt."

"But the Healing Crystal Unicorns

are close by," Emily said, waving over to them. "There's nothing to worry about."

But just then, they heard another cry. "Ouch! Oh my! Boo hoo!" A tiny unicorn bounced awkwardly towards them and Springer gave a cry of alarm. Emily knelt down beside the unicorn. It was rolling around in the grass, kicking its little legs. "Oh! It hurts! Help!"

The Healing Crystal Unicorns came cantering over.

"Where does it hurt?" Rosymane gasped, as she came to a stop. She was already reaching for her backpack of crystals.

"EVERYWHERE!" cried the little unicorn tearfully.

"Oh, you poor dear. Don't worry, we'll make it all better," Rosymane said. She reached over with a sparkling crystal gently held between her teeth. Her locket dangled from her neck and—

"Got it!" The unicorn lunged with teeth bared and grabbed the locket, tearing it from Rosymane's throat.

"Hey!" the girls shouted together.

As the creature sprang away, there was a zigzag of lightning followed immediately by a loud clap of thunder. As the smoke cleared, Emily and Aisha saw their worst nightmare.

Standing before them was Selena. And she'd stolen Rosymane's locket!

Chapter Three
A Halo of Stars

"Selena!" cried Queen Aurora in dismay.

Aisha folded her arms. "Selena, that's not yours!"

"Yes, give it back!" Emily added.

There was a sudden sound of rippling water from the stream and, before they knew what was happening, a slippery otter leapt out. It had a little black nose, brown fur on its back and white fur on its belly. The otter dripped water as it ran across the grass, scrambled up a tree stump and leapt – *one! two! three!* – across the backs of Ripplestripe, Twinkleshade and Firebright. With each leap there was

another sound, of a clasp being released, and three lockets fell – *one! two! three!* – to the ground, where the otter had already landed to catch them in his tiny paws. He swarmed across the grass to drop the lockets before Selena.

Emily darted towards the evil unicorn, but Selena scrambled back.

"How could you?" Aisha cried.

"Very easily," Selena snarled. "You lot were so slow off the mark, these are mine now." She put the lockets around her neck. "You don't get them back unless you make me queen."

Emily looked over at the little vampster who had just had his leg healed. "But that means ..."

"Yes! That no one in Enchanted Valley can be healed – of anything!" Selena cackled. "Come on, Slick!" she added,

beckoning to the otter.

"Selena, please!" said Queen Aurora, but Selena ignored her, knocking the queen over as she stormed past.

Aurora stumbled to one side. "Ouch!" she cried out. Her left foreleg twisted beneath her.

Selena and Slick bounced away over the fields.

Aurora fell to the ground in a heap. Emily and Aisha rushed to help Aurora, but it was clear that the queen's leg had been badly injured. When she tried to put some weight on the hoof, her leg buckled beneath her and she moaned with pain.

Emily glanced round desperately. "Rosymane! Are there any more crystals in your backpack?"

The unicorn trotted over. "Yes, but they won't work! Not now that we don't have our lockets." Her head dipped miserably, so that her pink nose nearly touched the ground.

Queen Aurora was biting her lip – Aisha could see that she was trying not to cry, but a single royal tear slid down her soft nose. Oh dear! Aisha put her arms around the queen's neck and gave her a

comforting hug. Emily came and did the same from the other side.

"Thank you, girls," Queen Aurora murmured.

But there was another crying noise starting up from behind them, and a thumping sound. When Emily glanced over her shoulder she saw Springer shaking his head.

"This is terrible!" he was saying. "No

one in Enchanted Valley will be safe! We can't do ANYTHING. What if we get injured?"

"We've helped get lockets back before," Emily said soothingly, "and we can do it again."

Springer stopped shaking his head. "Are you sure?"

Emily nodded firmly.

"Quite positive," said Aisha. "We're very good at rescuing lockets."

"Yes," said Emily, "everything will be all right. Won't it, Queen Aurora?"

All three of them turned to the queen, but she looked more sad than ever. She struggled to stand then walked slowly, limping on her bad leg.

"I'm afraid it's not that simple," she said. "This is Selena's worst trick ever."

"Why?" the girls asked together.

"Because the Crystal King is coming for a very important festival. Every year, the Healing Crystal lockets and all the healing crystals have to be magically recharged."

"Like batteries," Emily whispered to Aisha.

"It has to happen on the same day every year," Aurora continued, "and we have to have the Crystal King here to do the magic. The festival *has* to happen on time or ..." She trailed off, looking miserable.

"Or what?" Emily prompted.

"Or the crystals stop healing – for ever," Rosymane finished for the queen. Even as she finished speaking there was a small cry of pain from one of the fields and a gnome sat up on the grass, rubbing his head. Suddenly, Pillow Plains was starting to look less fun.

Aisha wasn't sure what to do next, but before she could ask the others, a shape appeared in the sky above them. For a moment, she worried that it might be Selena again, but instead, it was one of the most beautiful and noble unicorns the girls had ever seen. His coat was as white as snow, with a magnificent silver mane. Between his ears sat a small crown of crystals threaded in a wreath. It looked like he was wearing a halo of stars.

"Are you … the Crystal King?" Emily asked, bobbing a curtsey as he landed.

The unicorn's eyes crinkled in amusement. "I am indeed." He came and touched his nose to Emily's hand and then Aisha's. "I sense new friends."

He was right, of course. Any friend of Queen Aurora's was their friend too. But then he spotted the queen's limp leg and her sad face.

"My dear Aurora, what's wrong?" he asked quickly. The girls could tell that the king and queen were the closest of friends.

Aurora, the Healing Crystal Unicorns and the girls quickly filled him in on everything that had happened.

As they finished their story, the king's face clouded with concern. "We should go after Selena!" he said quickly.

Emily wasn't sure about that. If they needed the Crystal King's magic to recharge the healing lockets, then they couldn't risk putting him in danger. And besides … "Queen Aurora needs you," she said, pointing. The queen had limped over to the edge of the fields and was calling to the creatures to stop their fun.

"No more playing!" Her anxious voice floated over to them. "Everyone stop, now. It's too dangerous!" All around her were sad faces and slow steps as the creatures of Enchanted Valley abandoned their games. All but one …

"Look!" Aisha cried. A small, slippery figure with brown fur was still bouncing through the

air, moving away from the plains. "It's Slick!" There was a tiny glimmer around his neck. "He has one of the lockets."

"He helped Selena!" Emily quickly explained to the Crystal King.

"Then he must be caught," the king said.

"We'll do it," said Aisha, bravely. "You stay with Queen Aurora, Your Majesty."

The king frowned with concern. "Are you sure you can manage it?"

The girls exchanged a glance.

"Quite sure," said Emily. "We'll never let Selena win!"

The Crystal King dipped his head. "Then good luck. A king and queen are relying on you."

Chapter Four
Four Fabulous Friends

The girls were about to race off in the direction Slick had gone when Rosymane stepped forward. "I'll come with you," she offered. "The other Healing Crystal Unicorns should stay with the king and queen, but it's my locket Queen Aurora needs and I want to help find it."

"Thank you," Emily said. "Come on!"

The other Healing Crystal Unicorns wished them luck as the girls and Rosymane broke into a run. Emily and Aisha launched themselves into a purple field, and bounced on to the next one and the next – it was the quickest way of catching up with Slick. Rosymane flew

into the air, circling above their heads. The two girls jumped across the fields, then they felt some smaller bounces behind them. When they looked round …

"Springer!" Emily cried. For such a careful kangacorn, he was certainly leaping quite far.

"I want to help too!" he cried.

Aisha couldn't believe it! "Are you sure?" she asked. "It will be a big adventure. It might even be dangerous."

She waited for Springer to back away, and to say that he'd changed his mind. But no! He swallowed hard and took a step forward. "I love Enchanted Valley more than anything," he said. "I'll do whatever it takes."

Goodness, Aisha thought. *He's full of surprises*. But she was happy he wanted to come. The more help they had, the more chance they had of defeating Selena!

They reached the edge of the field, where Slick was bouncing on his bottom, pretending to make rude noises every time his bum hit the bouncy purple field.

"Hee, hee, hee!" He was laughing so hard and his tiny little ears flicked with delight. He didn't even realise that the friends had caught up with him. And there, looped around his neck, was Rosymane's locket!

Aisha didn't hesitate. She went into a forward roll that sent her leaping up – right on top of Slick. She threw her arms around him, but he was so slippery and wriggly that he shot out of her arms. Emily did the same, but he slid through her fingers like a wet bar of soap. She watched him bounce away towards the bottom of a hill. Aisha's mouth hung open in shock. Even her gymnastics skills hadn't helped her catch this naughty creature.

"I see where he gets his name from,"

she said as Emily helped her to her feet. "Slippery little otter!"

"We're not giving up yet," Emily said, waving to Springer. "Pincer movement! Come on!"

But Springer didn't move. "What's a pincer movement?" he asked.

Emily laughed and held up her hand in front of his face. Then she pinched her thumb and forefinger together, over and over. "It's like this," she said. "You come from one side and we come from the other and … pinch! We'll grab him between us!"

Springer nodded enthusiastically, and leapt to one side of the field as Emily ran to the other. Then, with a

"Wheeeeeeeeee!" they both slid down towards Slick, coming at him from either side and closing in. But at the last moment, Slick saw them and leapt away.

Aisha cried out as she saw Emily and Springer crash into each other in a jumble of limbs. She ran over to them. "Are you all right?"

Thankfully, Emily got up and dusted

herself off. "We're OK. Accidents happen!" she said, brightly.

Springer wasn't so happy. "That was awful!" he cried. "We shouldn't have done that." He shook his head in misery. "No, no, far too risky."

"Sometimes you have to take a chance," Emily said patiently.

"Sometimes you have to be brave," Aisha added.

Springer shook his head even more. "Sometimes it's best to be careful."

All three of them looked at each other.

"You're all right," said Rosymane as she landed next to them. "But Slick has gone." She pointed with her horn and they saw a little brown tail disappearing over the brow of one of the hills.

Emily sighed. "I don't think there's any point chasing him now."

"But we need to do something," said Aisha. "Queen Aurora is hurt."

The friends all gathered, their brows creasing as they thought hard.

Emily remembered the medicine cabinet back at home. It was full of plasters and bandages, cotton-wool balls and vitamin tablets. Even a bottle of golden cough syrup that looked just like a magic potion. Her face lit up. "What about Hob?" He was their hobgoblin friend, known for mixing wonderful potions in his cave. "Could he make something that would help Aurora?"

"I bet he could," Aisha said, fizzing with excitement.

"Climb on my back, I'll fly us there," Rosymane offered.

The girls scrambled up, but Springer held back, tapping his paws nervously. "I'm a bit afraid to fly," he admitted. "If we fall, we might get hurt."

"I promise I won't let you fall," said Rosymane calmly.

"All the same, I think I'd rather bounce," said Springer.

So they set off. Rosymane swooped over Enchanted Valley. The girls waved down to the tiny, bounding figure of Springer below.

"See you there!" Emily called.

Chapter Five
The Not Quite Perfect Recipe

Eventually, they spotted Hob's cave down below and came in to land. Springer arrived by their side, panting hard.

A figure appeared in the cave mouth – it was Hob!

"Welcome! Welcome!" he cried. "What can I do for you?"

Emily and Aisha shared a glance. Where should they begin? As quickly as they could they told him all about Serena's bad behaviour and Queen Aurora's injury.

"All the healing crystals have been stolen," Aisha said, finally. "And now we can't help the queen or her kingdom!"

"Unless …" Emily glanced past Hob, towards his cave, "… you have something?"

"Come on." Hob marched into the cave and everyone followed.

"It's very dark," Springer whispered. "We might trip over something."

But as they walked deeper underground, their eyes got used to the gloom. At the far end was a table, covered with equipment for potion-making. Bunches of herbs hung from the roof and candles flickered around the walls. There was a dresser full of jars and canisters. Hob ran a finger along a bookshelf,

looking for something.

"Yes! Here we are!" He reached for a huge, leather-bound book and brought it to the table. Then he licked a finger and flicked through the thick, yellow pages covered in tiny writing. Suddenly, he stopped and smoothed a hand over a page.

Emily and Aisha drew close and Aisha read out the strange, curly writing. "All-Better Butterscotch Drops." She felt her eyes light up with delight. "Perfect!"

But Hob was frowning at the recipe. "Sadly not." He stabbed a finger at the list of ingredients. "I don't have any sugar crystals."

Emily looked at his shelves. He was right. A large green jar labelled "*Sugar Crystals*" stood empty. She'd seen a jar like that before –

in the palace kitchen!

"Chef Yummytum could help!" she cried. "He might have some sugar crystals."

But Hob shook his head sadly. "Not like mine. My sugar crystals are magic, all the way from the Bonbon Forest."

Springer was hopping in excited circles. "I know it!" he said. "I can take us there!"

Hob smiled. "Excellent! I'll start making the potion. You go for the sugar crystals."

"It's a plan!" the girls cried.

Springer was already taking long hops out of the cave, but not too fast in case he bumped into something.

They burst out into the green valley and the girls scrambled on to a slab of rock and then up on to Rosymane's back. Emily held out a hand to help Springer up, but he shook his head.

"No flying for me," he said stubbornly. "Far too dangerous!" He bounded away across the grass and Rosymane launched

herself into the air to follow him.

Just past Hob's cave, they spotted a couple of tiny pixie figures. Rosymane flew lower and they could see that it was a pixie mother and her little baby daughter, in the garden of a neat little cottage. The mother pixie was holding on to the child's fingertips as the girl took some wobbly steps until with a sudden *plop!* her legs crumpled beneath her and she sat down hard on the ground. The girl's mouth opened in an 'O' of shock and she lifted her arms up to her mother, crying hard.

"Oh no, she's hurt herself!" Rosymane said.

The mother was carrying her child

inside. She was probably going to look for her healing crystals. But the crystals wouldn't work without the lockets! Rosymane flew lower and the girls called out to explain what had happened.

"We'll let you know when it's safe to play!" Emily finished. "Until then, be careful!"

The baby hid her face in her mum's shoulder, but the mother pixie waved and thanked them. She looked worried, and Aisha felt her own stomach grow tight with nerves.

"After we've got the sugar crystals, we have to find those lockets," she said grimly. "Not just for Queen Aurora, but for the whole kingdom!"

Chapter Six
Crystal Clouds

The air tasted sweet with sugar as they approached Bonbon Forest. The trees up ahead weren't green and brown, but a pure white, as if they had been dusted with snow.

Rosymane came in to land gently beside Springer.

"See?" The kangacorn bounded over to the edge of the forest. "I told you you'd be in good paws with me."

Aisha slid down off Rosymane's back and then so did Emily. They all fell silent as they entered Bonbon Forest. It was so beautiful here! The tree trunks were powdery white, like bonbons, and delicate branches of spun sugar rose above them. Each one had different coloured sugar crystals hanging from it, on thin golden stalks. They looked like sparkly fruit.

The girls looked at each other in delight. They'd entered a magical forest, spun from sugar!

Aisha and Emily went to the nearest tree and reached up to collect the sugar crystals, placing them carefully in paper bags that Hob had given them. It was like gathering cherries from Aisha's garden.

Just as Aisha was reaching for another sugar crystal, her hand froze in mid-air. "Look!" she whispered.

Emily followed where she was looking and spotted a tiny, glossy creature with brown fur that looked awfully like an otter.

"It's Slick!" Emily whispered back. "Perhaps he has Rosymane's locket!"

"Oh my goodness." Aisha's eyes grew wide. "If we can get the locket, we won't even need Hob's All-Better Butterscotch Drops!"

They crept closer through the maze of trees. Fortunately, the soft sugar coating on the ground muffled their footsteps. And besides, Slick was far too pleased with himself to notice anything. He was singing happily, and rolling around in the white powder.

"The perfect hiding place! Yes, it is – it is! Perfect for hiding a crystal locket." He leapt to his feet and gave one last look around the forest, before nodding to himself and scampering away.

The friends came out from the tree they'd been hiding behind. It was no good chasing after Slick – he'd already disappeared from sight.

Rosymane shook her mane. "He's right," she said sadly, "this is the perfect place to hide a crystal locket. There are so many sugar crystals here, it would be hard to make out the healing crystal locket."

Emily looked up at the treetops. "There aren't that many pink ones, though. I'm sure we can find it!"

The four of them moved carefully between the trees, looking for any sign of a rosy pink glow.

"There!" Emily ran over to a tangle of branches. A tiny pink crystal was hanging at the back. "Rosymane, could you fly and get it?"

Rosymane tried and failed to edge her nose between some sugar branches with syrup strung between them. "It's so thick and sticky in there," she said, "my body wouldn't make it through."

"Then one of us will have to climb," Emily replied. She looked hopefully at Aisha, who was a talented gymnast. Her friend was already starting to place a foot

on one of the lower branches.

"No!" cried Springer. "The branches are spun from sugar – it's too brittle and danger—"

Before he had chance to finish, the branch snapped beneath Aisha's foot, and fell into the powdery sugar below with a thump.

Aisha stepped back. For once, Springer was right to be so careful. The branches wouldn't take her weight.

"What shall we do?" Emily asked, looking back at the dangling pink crystal.

Rosymane shook her head sadly. "I don't know," she replied. "The healing crystal … it's too far out of our reach!"

The four of them gazed at the rosy

crystal as it bobbed in the breeze. There was silence all around them, other than the calls of Sugar Swallows. The birds flew in the air above them, scattering sweets over their heads.

"I could …" Springer began.

"Tell us!" the girls cried.

Rosymane gave him a slow nod of encouragement.

He swallowed hard. "I could try jumping for it."

"Oh, Springer. Are you sure?" Emily asked. "Wouldn't you be too scared?" He'd been scared of trampolines and of flying – he'd even been scared of going into Hob's cave.

Aisha took one of Springer's front paws

and patted it. "You don't have to make yourself do anything you don't want to."

But a determined look had settled on the kangacorn's face. "If it helps Enchanted Valley, I'll do it." He looked at the friends. "You've both shown me how to be brave."

The girls looked at one another. They felt proud of their new little friend.

"It would help the valley," said Emily.

"And we believe in you!" Aisha added. Anyone could be brave with their friends by their side.

Springer gave a final nod. "Stand back," he warned the girls.

It looked like a very complicated leap, and Springer looked very scared. Perhaps it was too big a jump for a little kangacorn.

Aisha and Emily linked arms and stood next to Rosymane. This was it! The moment Springer became a hero.

Chapter Seven
Ow, Ow, OW!

"Go, Springer, go!" the girls and Rosymane cried together.

Springer's furry brow creased in concentration as he stared at the tree. He shook out his limbs, one by one, getting them ready for a massive leap. Then he took one step, two steps backwards and launched himself into the air, sailing above the branches.

"Geronimo!" he cried.

His paws paddled through the air as his body drew an arc across the white, sugary forest. Then he reached out with a paw to swipe the crystal. The girls held their breath as they watched. The crystal bobbed and wobbled, and then it fell to the ground! Springer landed with a thump after it.

The girls rushed over. Aisha drew Springer into a hug. "Well done, Springer. Very well done," she whispered into his ear. Emily went to pick up the crystal, but when she held it out in the palm of her hand it looked soft and covered with a crust of sugar. She lifted it to her nose, then dropped her hand sadly.

"It isn't the crystal," she said. It reminded her of the glistening jellies in her grandma's box of treats at Christmas time.

Rosymane gently put her nose to Emily's hand and nibbled the crystal. "Definitely a sweet."

The girls could see Springer working hard to stay brave. "I'm sorry. I failed."

Aisha shook her head. "You haven't failed! It isn't your fault that wasn't the locket. We just have to carry on looking."

Both girls looked up to the treetops. They had to stay determined, for the sake of Enchanted Valley!

"Another one! Look!" Emily pointed higher up in the branches, where something sparkled brighter than any other crystal, with a warm glow as pink as Rosymane's coat. "There! I think that's the healing crystal."

She was right. She had to be! Springer had a second chance at being a hero!

"Stand back," he warned them again. They all scrambled out of his way. He took a run up and then – *boing!* – his strong back legs sent him out in a curving arc towards the highest branches.

He threw out a paw, reaching as far as it was possible for a kangacorn to reach.

Missed.

"No!" Emily, Aisha and Rosymane called out at the same time.

Springer landed and they saw his right back paw twist a little beneath him. "Ow! Oh, ow, ow, OW!" he cried.

The girls dashed over and knelt beside him.

"Springer, are you hurt?" Emily asked.

"My paw! I landed funny on it. Oh, it really does hurt." Springer's eyes were gleaming with tears.

Rosymane pawed the ground. "Oh, and I have no way to make you better. I'm so sorry, Springer!"

Aisha felt her heart shrink in her chest. Had they all come this far, only to fail? And Springer had been so brave, then hurt himself trying to help. And there was no way to heal him. It didn't seem fair! It felt as though everything was going wrong.

But then …

They caught a glimpse of dark brown fur amongst the white tree trunks. Slick was climbing a tree, reaching out his little otter paws towards the glow of the pink crystal.

"Quick!" Emily cried. She didn't care if Slick heard her now – this was too important.

Despite everything, a new look of

determination settled on Aisha's face. "Risky. But …"

Before anyone could stop her, she scrambled up the tree. The trunk felt slippery as ice beneath her feet, but her toes gripped on hard through her shoes. One foot after the other, hands holding on tight, she went higher and higher until she swung a hand out and felt her fingers close around the healing crystal.

"Yes!" she cried.

"No!" yelled Slick.

But then, with Slick wailing from a nearby branch, she heard a *snap!* and the world fell away beneath her. Aisha dropped the locket in shock.

She hadn't rescued the pink crystal. She'd failed, too. And as she fell through the air, all she could think was, *So close … So very close.*

But it was all over. In a tumble of limbs, she fell down, down, down. She waited for the hard bump of the ground.

Chapter Eight
Ready for Friends

But instead of a crash, Aisha fell into the soft, furry arms of – Springer!

"You saved me!" she said, as they landed back on the ground with a gentle bounce. "But your poor paw!"

Springer winced and sat back down. "It's OK, really," he said.

"You're a hero," Emily declared.

The healing locket fell into a soft pile of sugar beside Aisha. Slick jumped down to take it but Emily grabbed it just as Slick landed. Emily whipped her hand behind her back. Slick lunged for the locket, but he was too late.

"Got it!" Emily cried.

Slick was hopping from foot to foot. "Selena will be so angry with me!" He sounded desperate. "Please …" He held out a paw. "Please can I have it?"

Aisha felt a rush of pity for the creature. He never should have become Selena's helper. "I'm sorry," she said, "but it's back where it belongs."

Emily reached out and handed the

locket to Rosymane. The unicorn's horn lit up with happiness, sending soft rays of pink around the whole of Bonbon Forest. Aisha hadn't thought the forest could look any prettier, but it did now. The girls felt the world shift and settle around them. One part of Enchanted Valley had returned to order.

Rosymane reached into her backpack and touched a pink crystal to Springer's paw. Springer wiggled his toes in awe. "It's all better," he said. "And that was my biggest jump ever!"

"And you saved me from being hurt without thinking about your own safety. Thank you," Aisha said, stepping closer to stroke his fur. It was soft as a duckling's feathers, but she could feel the strong muscles beneath.

"You're very brave," Emily said, coming to stand beside him. She reached to pat his head but couldn't reach that far, so patted his arm instead. "We're proud of you."

Springer straightened up on his hind

legs. "I'm proud of myself," he said, in a surprised voice. "Maybe I don't need to be scared after all."

"Every adventure teaches you new things about your own abilities," Aisha said, nodding. "That's what we love about Enchanted Valley!"

"And now we'd better get back to Queen Aurora," said Emily. "Her leg has been hurt for a long time."

"Springer, would you like to fly on my back this time?" Rosymane shook herself with new energy – the girls could tell she was glad to be reunited with her locket.

The happiness was spreading. "Yes, please!" Springer cried, scrambling up on to her back. Slowly, Rosymane lowered herself to the ground, balancing Springer on her back. Aisha and Emily crept on too, and before they knew it – *whoosh!* – they were high in the air above Bonbon Forest.

They waved down madly. "Goodbye! Goodbye!" they called to the Sugar Swallows. The bonbon trees dipped and swayed, as though they were calling their own farewells.

Rosymane swept through the air. Then, time whizzing by, they arrived back at Pillow Plains. Below, they could see Queen Aurora lying on a cushion of soft moss. Her gentle face was still sad. The girls could tell her leg was still hurting. The Crystal King was next to the queen, watching over her.

Rosymane came down to land, settling into a gentle trot and then finally stopping before Queen Aurora and the Crystal King.

The friends slid from Rosymane's back.

Queen Aurora smiled when she saw them. "You've returned!"

"And you have the locket," the Crystal King said, beaming.

Rosymane trotted over and gently placed a crystal against Aurora's injured leg. Her locket glowed. Immediately, the queen gave a whinny of delight and a joyful leap. She was healed!

The girls began clapping. But before

either of them could say a word there was a flash of lightning and a figure appeared before them. Selena!

Emily thought she had never seen a face so screwed up with fury.

"That stupid Slick!" Selena cried. "He let me down!"

Right then, Emily wouldn't choose to be an otter for anything in the world. But as she watched, Selena's frown turned into a grin. "You'll never get the other lockets," Selena warned. "I'll still be queen."

"No, you won't," Aisha said bravely. "You don't deserve it."

"It's not up to you," Selena told the girls fiercely. "You don't even come from Enchanted Valley."

Emily stepped in front of her friend to protect her. “We belong here more than you do. At least we care about the creatures in this valley!”

“Caring? How boring!” Selena laughed. “Being a queen isn’t about caring. It’s about getting your own way the whole time and having a big comfy palace all to yourself.”

"You're wrong, Selena," said Queen Aurora calmly.

"And we'll never let you win," Aisha said.

Selena snorted in frustration, then she leapt back into the sky, and with a clap of thunder she flew away.

The girls dropped their arms to their sides as the air settled. Emily's hand knocked against something that rustled.

"Oh, no!" she cried, pulling out her paper bag of sugar crystals. "We haven't got these back to Hob."

Springer leapt forwards. "I can take them," he offered.

"If you're sure," Queen Aurora said. "There can never be too many All-Better

Butterscotch Drops."

Without a word, Springer took the bag and jumped away across Pillow Plains, bouncing with joy. He'd discovered what he was good at – being brave – and it was clear that he'd never look back. Not even to wave goodbye!

The girls went over to the queen.

"It's time for you to go home," she said gently.

Emily and Aisha nodded in understanding. "But we'll be back," they said. They both knew that this adventure couldn't be over until all the healing crystal lockets were returned to their unicorns.

Rosymane came to touch her nose to

each girl's hands. "Thank you," she said. "I couldn't have done this without you."

"None of us could," the Crystal King said. "I see why you are so important to Queen Aurora."

The girls felt themselves flush with pride, but then another feeling filled them as sparkles suddenly surrounded them and they lifted into the air … before coming back down in Aisha's garden.

"What shall we do next?" Aisha asked, glancing around.

"I think we've had enough adventures for one day." Emily wandered over towards a circle of daisies in the lawn. She settled down and began to gather some of the tiny white flowers into her lap, splitting a single green stem with her fingernail. She began to thread another daisy, and then another. She lifted her creation into the air. "Daisy chains?"

Aisha smiled and sat down beside her. "What an excellent idea."

The two of them sat quietly and made enough daisy chains for a bracelet and a necklace, then draped their creations around each other.

they heard joyful barking and a big SPLASH!

Emily laughed. “It’s Feather,” she said, pointing at the friendly dog. “He’s jumped in after his ball.” She waved to her next-door neighbour, Mr Pritchett.

Read

Firebright and the Magic Medicine

to find out what’s in store for Aisha and Emily!

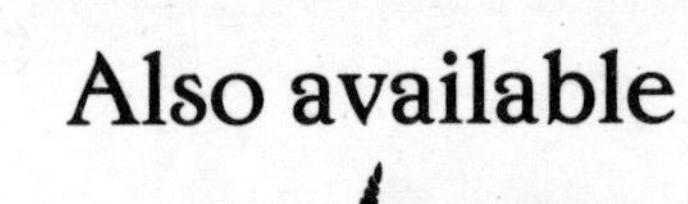

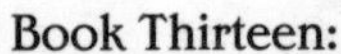

Book Fourteen:

Book Fifteen:

Book Sixteen:

Look out for the next book!

If you like
Unicorn Magic,
you'll love …

Welcome to Animal *Ark!*

Animal-mad Amelia is sad about moving house, until she discovers Animal Ark, where vets look after all kinds of animals in need.

Join Amelia and her friend Sam for a brand-new series of animal adventures!